Hiya! My name Thudd. Best robot friend of Drewd. Thudd know lots of stuff. How bug walk up wall. Why bubble break. How spider make web!

Drewd like to invent stuff. Thudd help! But sometime Thudd and Drewd make mistake. Invention plus mistake make adventure! Thudd and Drewd go on adventure now. Want to come? Turn page, please!

Get lost with
Andrew, Judy, and Thudd
in all their exciting adventures!

Andrew Lost on the Dog
Andrew Lost in the Bathroom
Andrew Lost in the Kitchen

AND COMING SOON!
Andrew Lost in the Garden

ANDREW LOST

3

IN THE KITCHEN

BY J. C. GREENBURG

ILLUSTRATED
BY DEBBIE PALEN

A STEPPING STONE BOOK™

Random House 🏠 New York

www.randomhouse.com/kids
www.AndrewLost.com

Library of Congress Cataloging-in-Publication Data
Greenburg, J. C. (Judith C.)
In the kitchen / by J. C. Greenburg ; illustrated by Debbie Palen.
    p. cm. — (Andrew Lost ; 3)
"A stepping stone book."
SUMMARY: After being shrunk by a shrinking machine, Andrew, his
cousin Judy, and Thudd the robot encounter drain flies, a cockroach,
and worse as they make their way through Mrs. Scuttle's house
toward safety.
ISBN 0-375-81279-2 (trade) — 0-375-91279-7 (lib. bdg.)
[1. Inventions—Fiction. 2. Size—Fiction. 3. Insects—Fiction.
4. Cousins—Fiction.]   I. Palen, Debbie, ill. II. Title.
PZ7.G82785 Ip 2002   [Fic]—dc21   2002007902

Printed in the United States of America
First Edition 10 9 8 7 6 5 4 3 2

*To Dan and Zack and Dad
and the real Andrew, with love.
—J.C.G.*

*To Dave, for washing the dishes.
—D.P.*

CONTENTS

ANDREW'S WORLD

Andrew Dubble

Andrew is ten years old, but he's been inventing things since he was four. His newest invention is the Atom Sucker. It shrinks things by sucking the space out of their atoms.

Andrew wanted to shrink himself so he could write a report about ants. But Andrew had a little accident. Now he, his cousin Judy, and his robot Thudd are so small they could use a drop of water as a swimming pool!

Judy Dubble

Judy is Andrew's thirteen-year-old cousin. She's pretty annoyed with Andrew for shrinking them. But Andrew shrank her parents' helicopter, too. If they can find it, she can fly them back to the Atom Sucker. But they have to hurry. In less than eight hours, the Atom Sucker will explode!

Thudd

Thudd is a little silver robot. The letters in his name stand for **The Handy Ultra-Digital Detective**. He's Andrew's best friend.

In the last book Thudd got soaked in a bathtub. He needs to get dry before his super-computer brain gets too soggy!

Uncle Al

Alfred Dubble is Andrew and Judy's uncle. He's a top-secret scientist. He invented Thudd!

Thudd has been trying to call Uncle Al

with his purple button, but his antennas are getting rusty. Andrew and Judy need to find some butter to grease Thudd's antennas, or Uncle Al won't be able to help them at all!

Harley

Harley is a basset hound. He belongs to Judy's next-door neighbor, but Judy is his best friend. After they were shrunk, Andrew, Judy, and Thudd ended up inside Harley's nose!

A few minutes ago, Harley pooped on the floor. When his owner cleaned it up, she cleaned up Andrew, Judy, and Thudd, too!

Mrs. Scuttle

Mrs. Scuttle is Judy's next-door neighbor. Harley belongs to her. She just flushed Harley's poop—together with Andrew, Judy, and Thudd—down the toilet!

 # 1 TOILET BOWLING

When you wake up in the morning, thought Andrew, *you never think about getting flushed down the toilet!*

At 12:01 that afternoon, Andrew had accidentally shrunk himself, his older cousin Judy, and his robot pal, Thudd. They were smaller than the point of a pin! Now they were huddled inside one of Andrew's inventions, the round, rubbery Umbubble.

The Umbubble was whirling round and round a toilet bowl. Judy's neighbor Mrs. Scuttle had just flushed it—along with a pile of poop from her dog, Harley.

"Cheese Louise!" said Judy. "It's like we're at the top of a water tornado!"

meep . . .

The sound came from the little silver robot that Andrew held tight in his hand. It was Thudd.

"Why do elephants got trunks?" Thudd asked. "Cuz they don't got pockets to put stuff in! Hee hee!"

Andrew looked at Judy. He was worried. Thudd had gotten wet in the bathtub. Now he was telling silly jokes.

The Umbubble picked up speed as it was pulled to the middle of the twisting water. Down, down, down they rushed! The light above them faded away.

meep . . . "'Fraid of dark!" said Thudd.

GLOOOGGHH! The toilet roared.

Judy leaned very close to Andrew. "If this thing springs a leak," she said, "I'm using

your head to plug it!"

The Umbubble slammed to a stop.

"*Yerggh!*" said Andrew.

"*Oof!*" said Judy.

"*Eek!*" said Thudd.

"We're stuck on something," said Andrew.

The roar of the water outside got softer and then stopped.

"I think all the water flushed," said Andrew.

Suddenly a light blinked in the darkness. It was the big purple button in the middle of Thudd's chest!

Snap!

The purple button popped open. A beam of light shot out. At the end of the beam floated a clear purple hologram of Andrew and Judy's Uncle Al.

"You're back!" said Andrew.

"Hey there!" said Uncle Al, smiling.

Andrew and Judy had talked to Uncle Al earlier that day. They were hoping he could help them somehow. But Andrew could tell

his uncle was worried. His bushy eyebrows were scrunched together.

"It's 5:15," Uncle Al said. "My plane is over Canada. I'm trying to get to you before 8:01, before the Atom Sucker—er—blows up. Where are you guys now?"

"We got flushed down the toilet," explained Judy. "Now we're stuck somewhere in the drainpipe."

"Good golly, Miss Molly!" said Uncle Al.

meep . . . "What is biggest ant on Earth?" Thudd interrupted. "Eleph-ant! Hee hee!"

"Uh-oh," said Uncle Al. "Thudd is telling elephant jokes. That means his thought chips are dangerously soggy! You've got to get him dry. And he needs to be rubbed with butter so he doesn't get rusty."

Judy frowned. "I know you can't see us when you're a hologram, Uncle Al. But we've got a big shortage of dryness and butter down here in the toilet!"

Uncle Al nodded. "What you need is a kitchen," he said. "The pipes that leave the toilet and the tubs and the sinks all connect to one big drainpipe."

meep . . . "Look!" said Thudd. His face screen lit up with a picture of the plumbing in Mrs. Scuttle's house.

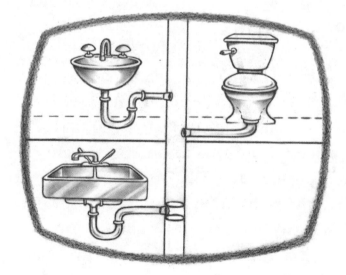

"I know," said Judy. "When I was a kid, I made real plumbing for my dollhouse."

"Super!" said Uncle Al. "So you know that connected to the big drainpipe is a smaller pipe that leads to the kitchen sink. Can you tell where you are in the big drainpipe?"

Andrew stuck Thudd to the sticky wall of the Umbubble. Then he unhooked his mini-flashlight from his belt and snapped it on.

The Umbubble was surrounded by mounds of gooey jelly! Stringy things were floating in the goo. Little blobs were squirming through it!

"We're stuck in slime like we saw in the bathtub drain," said Andrew.

"Ah, slime!" said Uncle Al. "I *love* that stuff! So interesting!"

Suddenly Uncle Al started disappearing, feet first. In an instant, all that was left of him was his shaggy hair.

"Uncle Al!" Judy yelled. "Don't go!"

But it was too late. He was gone!

 # **TRAPPED!**

"We've got to find the pipe to the kitchen," said Andrew. He waved his flashlight around the walls of the pipe. Huge, shiny water drops were trickling down over the slime.

"Wait!" said Judy. "I think I saw something!"

She grabbed the flashlight and pointed to a curving black shape below them.

meep . . . "Oody found place where kitchen pipe hook up with big drainpipe!" said Thudd.

"We need to get the Umbubble unstuck

and into that pipe!" said Judy.

"Jumping up and down might get us loose from the slime," said Andrew.

They bounced down on the Umbubble. Nothing happened. They bounced again. Slowly, the Umbubble pulled away from the slime.

"Yay!" Andrew cheered.

The Umbubble drifted down. Soon they were across from the dark hole where the pipes connected.

"I'll have to steer the Umbubble like I did when we were in the bathroom," said Judy.

Judy gave the flashlight back to Andrew and pulled a ballpoint pen from her pocket. She had taken the ink cartridge out of it before. She poked the empty pen tube through the wall of the Umbubble and started to blow.

The Umbubble moved in the opposite direction—into the new pipe.

"Woofers!" said Andrew. "This place smells like poop, old sneakers, and onions!"

Judy rolled her eyes. "Thanks for pointing that out," she said.

Andrew beamed his flashlight toward the top of the pipe. He spotted a cluster of strange, egg-like things clinging there. They were shiny and white. They looked squishy.

"I wonder what *those* are," said Andrew. He gave a little shiver. "But I kind of don't want to know."

meep . . . "Eggs of drain flies!" said Thudd. "Look!" Thudd pointed to an egg at the edge of the cluster. It was quivering! Suddenly it split open. Something started to wriggle out!

Judy stopped puffing to watch. "Looks like a worm!" she said.

meep . . . "Baby drain fly," said Thudd. "This how it look when it grow up!" Thudd pointed to his face screen.

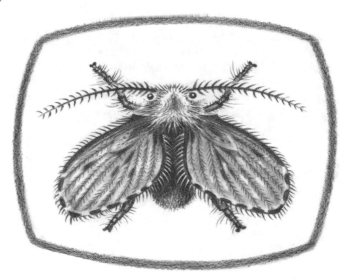

Andrew and Judy were staring at Thudd's screen when the Umbubble bumped into something. Andrew shined his flashlight on it. There was a turn in the pipe. It was going down. And the pipe below was filled with water!

"What's this?" said Andrew. "I thought the pipe would turn up toward the sink."

"We've come to the trap in the drain," said Judy.

"Why would anyone put a trap in a drain?" asked Andrew.

Judy gave Andrew her *don't-you-know-anything* look. "Pipes under sinks and toilets and tubs all have these U-shaped parts to trap water," she said. "The water keeps the stinky smells from getting into the house."

Andrew scratched his head. "You mean we have to dive through that water to get to the sink?" he asked.

"Not just water," said Judy. "Anything

that goes down the drain gets stuck in the trap. Mushy meat, moldy mushrooms, gunky grapes. . . ."

"Okay, okay!" Andrew said.

Judy let the Umbubble drift down. Below them floated dark chunks and shiny, slimy things.

Then Andrew's light flashed on something familiar sticking out of the water. It was something thick and scaly.

"It's a hair!" said Andrew.

"Mrs. Scuttle has long hair," said Judy. "If it's one of hers, we could follow it through the trap to the sink. But wait a minute." Judy's eyes got narrow. "We'll have to stick our hands into the yucky stuff to grab the hair!"

Andrew and Judy looked at each other. Andrew was about to ask Thudd if he had a better idea when he heard a sound he didn't want to hear.

"Shnurm . . . shnurm . . . shnurm . . ."

Thudd was snoring again! Sleeping was *another* thing Thudd had never done before he got wet.

Judy yanked the pen tube out of the Umbubble. Then she rolled up the sleeves of her jacket. Andrew stuck his flashlight on the wall of the Umbubble next to Thudd.

"Ready?" asked Judy.

Andrew nodded.

They poked their hands through the rubbery Umbubble and reached out into the gooey darkness.

3 PIPE DOWN!

"Yeuuuw!" said Judy. "It's so *squishy* out there. I haven't done anything this disgusting since I ate a fried cricket in Australia."

"Don't think about it," said Andrew.

They grabbed on to the hair and began to pull the Umbubble down into the goop.

Mushy shapes moved like ghosts in the darkness outside the Umbubble.

"Andrew, look!" said Judy, pointing. "It's one of your initials!"

A white letter *A* was floating by outside.

"And there's a *B*!" she continued.

"I guess Mrs. Scuttle likes alphabet soup," said Andrew.

Then an enormous green flower the size of a dump truck floated up through the letters.

"Bizarre-o!" said Judy.

meep . . . "Broccoli flower!" said Thudd, awake again.

Suddenly the beam from the flashlight caught a sparkle of color outside. It flashed

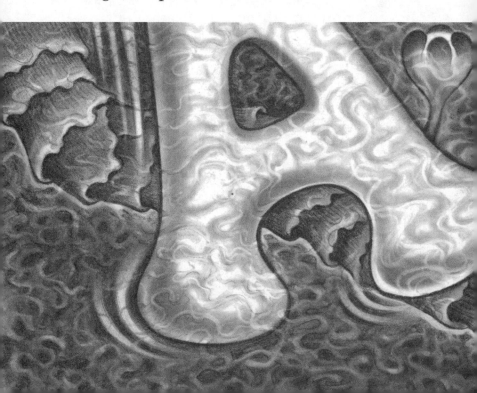

red and yellow and blue and white.

"Wowzers!" said Andrew.

Judy leaned over to see. "It looks like part of a rainbow!" she said.

Thudd pressed the "What's It?" button on his chest, and a thin red ray shot out at the twinkling thing. The "What's It?" ray told Thudd what things were made of.

meep . . . "Diamond!" said Thudd. "Diamond made of stuff inside pencils!"

"It sure doesn't look like pencil lead," said Andrew.

meep . . . "Diamond come from deep inside Earth," said Thudd. "Hot, hot, hot! Pencil stuff get squished into diamond!"

Andrew looked at Judy. "Maybe Mrs. Scuttle is always grumpy because she lost her diamond ring."

Judy shook her head. "Mrs. Scuttle would be grumpy if she had a diamond as big as a barn."

They dragged the Umbubble past the diamond. The underwater world was quiet and spooky. There was no way to tell where they were, or if the hair would lead them all the way through the trap.

Andrew squinted. It seemed that the icky blackness all around them was turning into yucky grayness.

"Wowzers!" said Andrew. "It's getting lighter!"

Judy pushed her face close to the wall of the Umbubble. "I think we're getting close to the top of the trap!" she said.

Andrew and Judy pulled the Umbubble along the hair faster.

At last the Umbubble popped to the top of the water.

"Yay!" cheered Andrew.

"Yeep!" squeaked Thudd.

"We did it!" said Judy.

The Umbubble was covered with slimy, seaweedy gunk from the trap. But there were a few places where they could see out.

Andrew pointed at a circle of light above the Umbubble. "It's the kitchen drain!" he said.

"Now the problem is to get there," said Judy. "Help me pull the Umbubble a little further up."

Once they were off the water, Judy and Andrew pulled their arms back into the Umbubble.

Andrew wiped his slimy hands on his pants. "Super gross!" he said.

"We've won the lottery of grossness," said Judy.

Judy got out her pen tube again and pushed it through the bottom of the Umbubble. She looked at Andrew.

"Okay, Disaster Master," she said, "it's your turn to blow the Umbubble."

"Sure," said Andrew. He started to blow. They floated up.

Thwunk!

The Umbubble had bumped into something.

"It's probably the side of the pipe," said Judy.

Andrew puffed and puffed, but he couldn't make the Umbubble move.

"We're stuck again!" said Judy.

Andrew stopped puffing. The Umbubble started moving. But it wasn't floating. It was sort of . . . scampering!

Judy and Andrew tried to find clear spots on the Umbubble wall to see what was going on.

"I see a hairy tree branch," said Judy.

"I see a wall of shiny tiles," said Andrew.

Suddenly Thudd's antennas started twitching. Thudd used his antennas to hear. He also used them to smell with. Something was making them wiggle!

# THAT SINKING FEELING

"*Eek! Eek!*" Thudd squeaked. "Smell something big! Bad!" His antennas were going crazy. "Cockroach!"

Thudd pulled himself off the Umbubble wall and scuttled over to Andrew.

meep . . . "Shiny tiles are cockroach eye!" Thudd said. "Cockroach eye made of two thousand little eyes. But they not see much. Mostly just see when stuff move."

"And what's this hairy tree branch thing?" asked Judy.

Thudd hurried over to Judy's side.

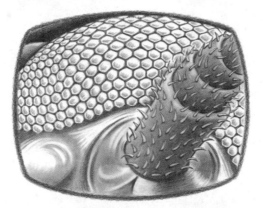

meep . . . "Antenna," said Thudd. "Antenna taste stuff. Antenna feel stuff move."

The circle of light above them was getting bigger.

"I think the cockroach is climbing into the sink," Judy said.

meep . . . "When cockroach get to kitchen," said Thudd, "cockroach look for food. Then hide. Go find big cockroach family behind wall."

"Then we'd better dump this bug," said Judy, "before we end up having Thanksgiving dinner with a *cockroach* family!"

Judy jostled against the wall of the Umbubble. Andrew did, too. But they couldn't get loose.

Then the cockroach twitched its antenna. The Umbubble floated free! The cockroach scrambled up the drain ahead of them.

Andrew shut off his mini-light and attached it to his belt loop. Then he got back to blowing the Umbubble to the circle of light.

At last they popped into the sink. It was a skyscraper city of dirty dishes!

Eeeeeee! came a loud screech.

Judy covered her ears. "What's *that*?" she asked.

Andrew shook his head. Then he heard softer clicking sounds. "*That* sounds like—"

meep . . . "Harley paws on kitchen floor!" Thudd said.

Thump! Thump! Thump! came heavy footsteps. Mrs. Scuttle's voice shook the Umbubble. "Harley, you bad dog!" she yelled. "How *dare* you poop on the floor!"

Ahwoooo! Harley howled.

"*No!*" Mrs. Scuttle shouted. "You're *not*

going out! You'll head straight for the garbage again. Right after I've given you a bath, too! You've already wrecked my day and my bathroom!"

Judy sighed. "Mrs. Scuttle doesn't deserve a great dog like Harley," she said.

Andrew blew the Umbubble up through the pile of dirty dishes. On a white plate below them, they saw the yolk of a fried egg. It looked like a sun that had crash-landed in a desert of toast crumbs.

Near the egg yolk, a chunk of apple was turning brown.

meep . . . "What is difference between fire and brown apple?" asked Thudd.

"I don't know," said Andrew.

meep . . . "Not a lot!" said Thudd. "Fire happen when stuff get together with oxygen fast! Brown apple happen when stuff get together with oxygen slow."

Thudd pointed to a huge tangle of rusty

wire at the bottom of the sink. It was a steel-wool pad for scrubbing dirty pots.

meep . . . "Rusty thing on slow fire!" said Thudd.

If we don't find some butter soon, thought Andrew, *the same thing could happen to Thudd.*

EEEEEEE! The screech was still going on, only now it was louder and higher.

"It's worse than chalk on a blackboard!" Judy complained.

The Umbubble floated out of the sink. Now they could see the whole kitchen.

Next to the sink, the kitchen counter was piled high with fruits and vegetables.

Next to the counter was the stove. Andrew realized that was where the screech was coming from. It was a teakettle! Mrs. Scuttle lifted it off the stove.

"I'd better have my cup of tea before the next disaster," she said to herself.

meep . . . "When water boil, little water

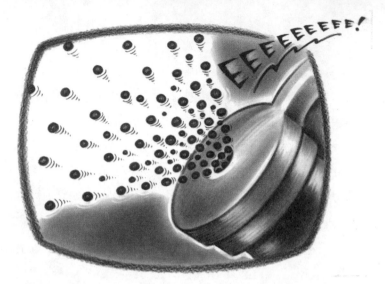

molecules get lots of energy from heat! Go off into air. Sound happen when lotsa molecules rub against spout of kettle!"

They watched Mrs. Scuttle pour steaming water from the teakettle into a big white mug. On the other side of the room, Harley got up on his hind legs and pushed his front paws against the screen door. It creaked and flew open.

"Harley! No!" yelled Mrs. Scuttle as she rushed over to grab him.

It was too late. Harley escaped!

But other things came in.

BYE-BYE, UMBUBBLE!

Bzzzzzz!

Big black flies zoomed through the open door. Mrs. Scuttle hurried over and slammed it shut.

Slamming the door sent a little gust of wind through the kitchen. It caught the Umbubble and sent it spinning toward the kitchen counter.

"Hang on!" said Judy. "We're going to crash into Veggie Mountain!"

Andrew grabbed Thudd and shoved him into his shirt pocket. He saw a wall of red and smelled a familiar, spicy smell. Then the Umbubble crashed. Thorns pierced the wall of the Umbubble everywhere!

"Yikes!" hollered Andrew. "The Umbubble is shredding!"

The Umbubble collapsed around them like a party balloon. They were caught on a tomato stem. It was as thorny as a monster cactus!

Then Andrew saw something move. A pair of long, hairy antennas twitched at the bottom of the tomato.

"Holy moly!" said Andrew. "The cockroach!"

Judy snapped off two prickles from the tomato stem and gave one to Andrew. "If it comes this way, use this!" she said.

"Um, thanks," said Andrew. "But this thing is about as scary as a speck of dust!"

"Do you have a better idea, Mr. Smarty-Pants?" asked Judy.

The cockroach played its antennas over a strawberry that was next to the tomato.

meep . . . "Strawberry only fruit that have seed on outside!" said Thudd.

Judy rolled her eyes. "That might be interesting, Thudd," she said, *"if we weren't about to be devoured by an enormous insect!"*

The cockroach started to climb up the tomato. Andrew, Judy, and Thudd stared down at two walls of cockroach eyes. The cockroach's jaws snapped like giant, jagged scissor blades in front of them.

Andrew and Judy waved their tomato prickles. The cockroach didn't seem impressed.

meep . . . "Cockroach not like light," said Thudd. "Get flashlight, Drewd!"

But before Andrew could grab it, there was a flash of yellow.

THWAAAP!

The cockroach was gone!

Andrew looked up to see Mrs. Scuttle

waving a banana and searching the sink.

meep . . . "Cockroach too fast for human," said Thudd. "Got antennas in rear end that tell when stuff move."

"Like having eyes in back of your head," said Andrew.

"Like having eyes in your behind!" said Judy.

Mrs. Scuttle was muttering again. "First, my dog gets in the garbage. Then there's ants in my bathtub and spiders on my ceiling. Now there's a cockroach in my sink! I can't take it anymore. I've *got* to calm down."

Mrs. Scuttle put down the banana and took a sip of tea. "I know!" she said. "I'll make myself a teensy-weensy grilled cheese and tomato sandwich! Yes!"

"*No!*" said Andrew and Judy together.

"We've *got* to get off of this tomato!" said Judy.

She started to climb through the thorny

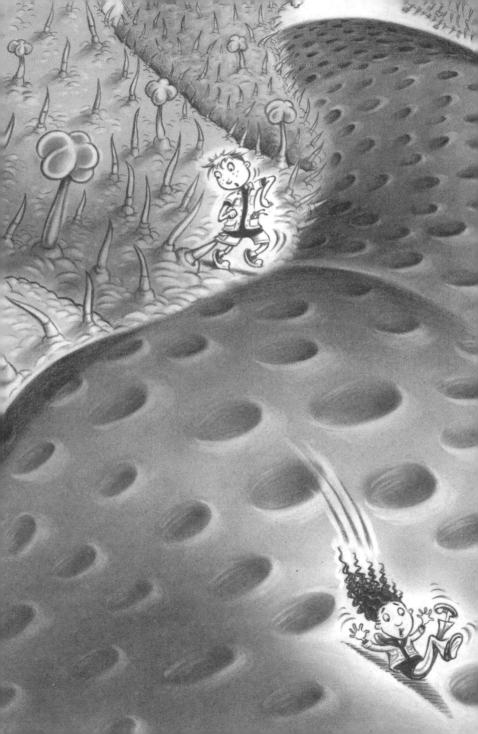

spikes of the tomato stem. Andrew followed. But it was like climbing down a cactus.

"She'll be comin' round the mountain when she comes," sang Mrs. Scuttle. She slipped a slice of bread onto a blue plate. Then she slapped a slice of orange cheese on top of the bread.

Her giant fingers grabbed Andrew and Judy's tomato. Andrew's shorts got caught on the tomato prickles!

"She'll be comin' round the mountain, she'll be comin' round the mountain, she'll be comin' round the mountain when she comes!" sang Mrs. Scuttle.

Judy jumped off the tomato stem and started sliding down the tomato skin. She was almost out of sight!

Andrew tugged his shorts free from the prickles and hurried after her. The tomato skin was smooth but dotted with bowl-shaped craters. He jumped onto it and started sliding.

Then there was a flash right above him. A gleaming wall of silver slammed down between him and Judy!

SPLITTING UP!

Mrs. Scuttle's knife chopped the tomato in half. Andrew and Judy were caught on opposite sides!

Andrew peered toward the other half of the tomato. Mrs. Scuttle was slicing it! She plopped three dripping slices onto the cheese-covered bread.

Then Mrs. Scuttle shook some salt onto the tomato slices and laid a piece of bread on top of them.

"Now I'll get my little sandwichy into the oven," she said. "Mmm-mmm-mmm!"

She glanced at the microwave oven and then at the toaster oven. "Eeny meeny miney moe. . . ."

meep . . . "All food got water inside," said Thudd. "Microwave make water molecules flip around fast, fast, fast! Get hot, hot, hot! Then water molecules make other molecules hot. Toaster oven work different. Make all molecules hot."

"I think I'll use the microwave," said Mrs. Scuttle. "It's faster!"

She grabbed the sandwich off the plate and popped it into the microwave oven. She set the timer and turned the oven on.

"Oh no!" yelled Andrew. "If Judy's on that sandwich . . ."

"Oody!" whimpered Thudd. His eyes closed. *"Shnurm . . . shnurm . . . shnurm . . ."* Thudd was snoring again.

"I'd better put the rest of this tomato in the fridge," said Mrs. Scuttle.

The kitchen became a blur as Mrs. Scuttle whisked Andrew's half of the tomato away and opened the refrigerator door.

From the edge of the tomato, Andrew saw the top shelf of the refrigerator. It was crowded! There were bottles of orange soda, a carton of milk, and a cooked turkey. Jars of jelly and mustard and mayonnaise were piled on top of each other.

"Hmm," mused Mrs. Scuttle. "There isn't room for another crumb in this refrigerator."

Mrs. Scuttle leaned down to the middle shelf. It was jammed, too. There were jars of pickles and olives, a water jug, and chocolate cupcakes. In the center of the shelf sat a big cabbage with part of its top cut off.

"I guess this will have to do," said Mrs. Scuttle.

She set Andrew's half of the tomato on top of the cabbage and slammed the refrigerator door shut. The light in the refrigerator went

off. Jars and bottles clanked against each other. The cabbage tipped, and Andrew's tomato slid to the edge of the cabbage and bumped into a jar of pickles.

Andrew shivered. It was cold! He snapped his flashlight on.

Splot!

A big drop of something plopped down onto the tomato.

meep . . . "Whazzit?" Thudd said as he woke up.

Andrew shined his light up. The milk carton was above them.

"It must be leaking," said Andrew.

meep . . . "Milk mostly water," said Thudd. "Milk white cuz of little protein blobs and little fat blobs. Milk got germs, too. Milk alive!"

Andrew beamed his flashlight at the bottom shelf of the refrigerator.

Far below, he could see an open carton of yogurt, a bowl of eggs, and a half-eaten sandwich on a glass plate. There was a wedge of cheese with blue streaks running through it. And then Andrew spied it.

"Super-duper pooper scooper!" he said. "Look, Thudd! A stick of butter!"

meep . . . "Why did elephants get thrown out of pool?" asked Thudd. "Not keep trunks up! Hee hee!"

Thudd's big purple button began to blink. It snapped open, and Uncle Al appeared at the end of a thin purple beam.

"Hey there!" said the Uncle Al hologram. "I tried to stay with you last time, but Thudd's antennas are starting to rust. I'm reaching you with a high-power hologram. Where are you now?"

"We're in Mrs. Scuttle's refrigerator," said Andrew.

"Good work!" said Uncle Al. A proud smile spread across his face. "I *knew* you'd find a way to get into the kitchen! Any progress with getting Thudd buttered up? If his antennas get rustier, I won't be able to reach you."

"There's some butter on the refrigerator shelf below us," said Andrew. "But I don't know how we can get it."

Uncle Al grinned. "I think I have an idea . . . ," he said.

THE DRASTIC ELASTIC

"What are you wearing today?" asked Uncle Al.

"Well, um, I'm wearing my blue shorts and that great safari shirt you gave me," said Andrew. "The one with all the pockets."

"Perfect!" said Uncle Al. "Remember, Andrew, most answers are in your head or in your pockets—sometimes both! When I gave you that shirt, I put a surprise in a secret pocket. It's under the left side of your collar. It's a new thing I've been working on. The Drastic . . ."

Suddenly Uncle Al's voice faded away. So did the rest of Uncle Al!

Andrew checked his collar. There was a little zipper on the left side. He unzipped it and found a tiny pocket. But there was nothing there!

Then Andrew remembered that Uncle Al, smart as he was, sometimes got left and right mixed up. So Andrew checked the right side of his collar. There was another secret pocket. This time there was something in it.

It felt like a tiny, squooshy lump. Andrew unzipped the pocket and took it out. It looked like a piece of rubber band with a tiny cup at each end.

There was a tag attached to it. It said THE DRASTIC ELASTIC, VERSION 1.1.

meep . . . "Let go of end," said Thudd.

Andrew held one end of the Drastic Elastic and let go of the other end. It fell through the grating of the middle shelf and stretched all the way to the bottom of the refrigerator!

"Wowzers schnauzers!" yelled Andrew. "This is the stretchiest thing I've ever seen!"

Andrew tried to pull the end back up, but the Drastic Elastic just seemed to get longer and longer.

meep . . . "Yank, Drewd!" said Thudd. "Like yo-yo!"

Andrew yanked the end of the Drastic Elastic. The other end came whizzing back!

"Jumping gerbils!" said Andrew.

Andrew tied one end of the Drastic Elastic around Thudd.

"Okay!" said Andrew. "I'll get you down to the butter, Thudd. You grab a big hunk. Then I'll snap you back and get you buttered!"

"Yoop! Yoop! Yoop!" said Thudd.

Thudd jumped off the tomato and whizzed down to the bottom shelf. He landed in the bowl of eggs.

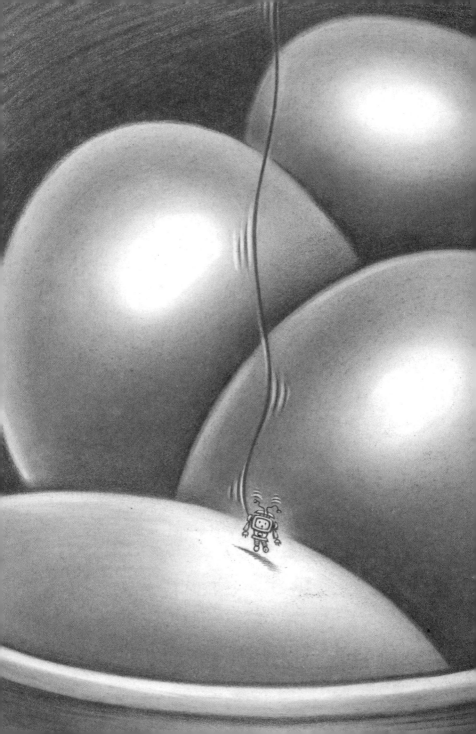

"Are you okay, Thudd?" Andrew called down.

But Thudd couldn't hear him. His voice was too tiny to hear from so far away.

Then Andrew remembered the little cups at the ends of the Drastic Elastic. He held his cup to his mouth.

"Hey, Thudd!" he said. "Can you hear me?"

Down below, Thudd spoke into his end. "Yoop, Drewd!"

"Thudd, I'll try to swing you off the eggs and onto the butter," said Andrew.

meep . . . "Know why egg not round like ball?" asked Thudd.

"Thudd, it's not a good time to start explaining stuff," said Andrew. "We've got to get you buttered up. And then we've got to rescue Judy."

meep . . . "If egg round, egg roll away easy," Thudd continued. "Egg get broke. Get lost. Oval-shape egg not roll away easy."

"Thudd, I'm going to pull you off those eggs right now," said Andrew. "Get ready!"

meep . . . "Eggshell got little holes!" said Thudd, beaming a picture up to Andrew. "When egg got chick inside, chick get air!"

"Enough of that, Thudd!" said Andrew.

Andrew tugged Thudd off the eggs and tried to swing him onto the butter. But Thudd landed on the half-eaten sandwich and tumbled into a deep bread crater.

meep . . . "Bread got lotsa holes like moon," said Thudd. "Hole in moon made by meteor. Hole in bread made by little yeast things. Live in bread dough." Thudd beamed Andrew a picture of yeast.

"Little yeast thing eat stuff in dough," Thudd said. "Then yeast burp! Burp make bubble in dough. Bread get cooked. Little yeast thing die. Bubble stay!"

Andrew shivered. "Come on, Thudd," he said. "My fingers are getting awfully cold."

Thudd climbed out of the bread crater.

meep . . . "What is gray and got four legs and trunk?" asked Thudd. "Mouse on vacation. Hee hee!"

Andrew sighed. "I'm going to try again to get you over to the butter. Try to swing yourself that way."

"Okey-dokey!" said Thudd.

Andrew finally got Thudd swinging over the butter. He was just about to land Thudd on the creamy yellow surface when the refrigerator door flew open.

8 BUTTER UP!

"Tum, tee dee tum tum . . . ," sang Mrs. Scuttle. Her nose appeared in front of Andrew like a big pink ski slope.

"Now, where are those pickles?" she asked herself. "Oh, here!"

Meaty Scuttle fingers wrapped themselves around the jar of pickles that Andrew's tomato was leaning against. The tomato wobbled on the edge of the cabbage. Andrew turned off his flashlight, clipped it back onto his belt loop, and held on!

Rrrrrrrrrinnng! Rrrrrrrrinnng! Rrrrrrrrrinnng!

It was Mrs. Scuttle's phone.

"I'll bet that's the mayor calling me back!" said Mrs. Scuttle.

She slammed the refrigerator door shut. But she slammed it so hard that it sprang open again!

"Well, *hello*, Mayor Zamboni!" said Mrs. Scuttle. Her voice had turned sticky sweet. "It's about my neighbors, the Dubbles. Yes, I've called about them many times."

Splot!

A drop of milk landed right on top of Andrew. It washed him over the edge of the slippery tomato skin!

"Woofers!" said Andrew. He clung to the edge of the slippery tomato with one hand and the Drastic Elastic with the other!

Mrs. Scuttle's voice got less sweet. "I'm a very busy person, Mayor Zamboni, but I am certainly *not* a busybody!" Mrs. Scuttle was silent for a moment. "I can't believe it!" she finally said. "He hung up on me!"

Andrew's cold fingers just couldn't hold on. He fell off the tomato and landed softly on a yellow snowdrift—the stick of butter!

Up above, the tomato was slipping farther and farther over the edge of the cabbage. Finally, it toppled off the cabbage, bombed down past the middle shelf, smacked into the glass plate with the half-eaten sandwich, and . . .

Craaack!

The whole mess crashed to the kitchen floor.

Andrew heard Mrs. Scuttle's heavy footsteps thumping nearer. "This is the last straw!" she screamed.

Andrew looked around for Thudd. He couldn't see him, but he still had one end of the Drastic Elastic. "Thudd!" Andrew called. There was no answer.

Andrew snapped the Drastic Elastic.

Thudd came skimming toward him across the butter!

"*Shnurm* . . ." Thudd had fallen asleep again. All his buttons were blinking red.

"Wake up, Thudd!" said Andrew. He untied Thudd from the Drastic Elastic. Then he scooped up a handful of butter and started rubbing Thudd all over, especially his antennas.

The refrigerator door opened wide. Mrs. Scuttle got down on her hands and knees to clean up the mess. The top of Mrs. Scuttle's head was right across from Andrew. He could see the dark roots of her hair, even some dandruff!

"*Shnurm* . . . Butter made from lotsa little fat globs in milk . . . *Shnurm* . . ." Thudd was talking in his sleep!

As Andrew rubbed Thudd with butter, Thudd's buttons went from blinking red to yellow. Then Thudd opened his eyes!

"Now I've got a headache!" Mrs. Scuttle groaned. She looked at her watch. "Heavens to Betsy! It's 6:30! How am I ever going to get ready for my garden party tonight?"

Mrs. Scuttle's grumpy face rose past Andrew like a balloon in the Thanksgiving Day Parade.

meep . . . "What is big as elephant but weigh nothing?" asked Thudd. "Elephant shadow! Hee hee!"

"Oh no!" said Andrew. "You're still telling elephant jokes!"

meep . . . "Still soggy!" said Thudd. "Got to get dry!"

Bing!

"The microwave!" said Mrs. Scuttle. She ran over to the microwave oven and flung it open. The door was spattered with orange cheese and red tomato!

"I can't believe it!" she said. "I must have set it for ten minutes by accident! Another mess!"

Mrs. Scuttle shook her head. "I should just go back to bed," she groaned. "But I've got to have something to eat. Maybe just a slice of toast with my tea. That's it! Hot buttered toast!"

A PATCH OF BLUE

Oh no! Andrew thought. He grabbed Thudd and started to run toward the edge of the butter. But it was far away, and the butter was slippery.

Mrs. Scuttle opened the door of the toaster oven, put in a slice of bread, closed the door, and flipped a switch.

Then she stomped back to the refrigerator. The next second, Andrew and Thudd were zooming out of the refrigerator into the warm air of the kitchen. It was as if the butter dish were a flying saucer!

They landed on the kitchen counter, right next to the plate where Mrs. Scuttle had made her tomato-and-cheese sandwich.

Ding!

Mrs. Scuttle took the hot toast out of the toaster oven and put it on the plate.

Then Andrew saw a silver flash. It was the knife again!

The blade slammed into the stick of butter and peeled the butter away in a huge wave of yellow. It curled toward Andrew and Thudd, picked them up, and swept them away!

WHOA!

They lifted off into the air and then swooped down. Andrew could see they were headed for the huge brown field of toast below!

The butter landed, and Andrew began to feel warm—*toasty* warm.

meep . . . "Warm, warm, warm!" squeaked Thudd. "Getting dry!"

Andrew smiled. "Super-duper pooper scooper!"

The butter was melting. Andrew was getting as buttery as Thudd! The knife started smooshing the butter around the bread like a snowplow. Andrew and Thudd ended up on the very edge of the bread crust.

Andrew looked down over the bread crust to the plate below. He saw lots of breadcrumbs and some sparkling, cube-shaped boulders.

meep . . . "Salt!" said Thudd. "Salt come from salt cave. Salt cave happen when old ocean dry up!"

Then Thudd got excited.

meep . . . "Look!" he squeaked. "Blue!"

Andrew squinted in the direction Thudd was pointing. There was a speck of blue behind one of the salt boulders. Above the blue was a bit of frizzy brown!

"Judy!" said Andrew.

"Oody!" said Thudd.

Judy didn't look up. She was too far away to hear their tiny voices.

"Hmm," murmured Andrew. "I have an idea."

He threw the end of the Drastic Elastic toward Judy. It zoomed past her and bounced off a salt crystal. Judy spun around to see what had happened. Then she looked up. But she didn't see them.

Andrew snapped the Drastic Elastic back. He whirled it over his head like a lasso and threw it again. This time the little cup on the end got caught on a salt crystal next to Judy.

Judy ran over to the cup. She picked it up and looked it over. Then she put it up to her mouth. Andrew put the other end up to his ear.

"WELL, HELLO, MR. BUG-BRAIN!" Judy yelled. She yelled so loudly that Andrew's ear hurt! "Wait till I get my hands on *you*! Where have you *been*?"

"We've been chilling in the refrigerator," said Andrew. "But the good news is that Thudd got buttered. And the toast is so warm it's getting him dry! What happened to *you*? We were afraid you got microwaved on Mrs. Scuttle's sandwich!"

"Almost!" said Judy. "But I got knocked off a slice of tomato by a grain of salt!"

Suddenly the toast started rising into the air. Mrs. Scuttle was about to take a bite!

Andrew felt a tug on the Drastic Elastic. Judy was trying to pull them off the crust and down to the plate. But the Drastic Elastic was caught on the crust!

Judy got dragged off the plate as Mrs. Scuttle raised the toast to her lips. Andrew yanked the Drastic Elastic free from the crust and gave it a sharp snap. Judy bounced up and landed beside him!

"Oh, great!" said Judy. She let go of her end of the Drastic Elastic and climbed over a buttery crumb. "Now we're *both* going to be slurped up by rubbery Scuttle lips!"

10 BUZZING OFF

The slice of toast paused in midair while Mrs. Scuttle took a sip of tea.

Bzzzzzz . . .

Andrew looked up to see a humongous, hairy fly dive-bombing the toast! The next thing they knew, Andrew and Judy were staring at two gigantic, glistening domes!

meep . . . "Fly eyes!" said Thudd. Then he pointed at the fly's hairy feet. "See claw? Help fly climb. Fly got hairy foot pad. Make fly stick to slippery thing. Walk on glass! Walk on wall! Walk on ceiling! Fly taste with foot pad, too!"

A long, thick, rubbery tube uncurled from beneath the fly's eyes.

meep . . . "Fly mouth!" said Thudd.

Something watery drooled out of the tube.

"*Ewww!*" said Judy. "What's it doing?"

meep . . . "Fly not eat solid stuff," said Thudd. "Fly throw up on food first. Turn food to mush. Fly suck mush through tube."

"*EWWW!*" said Judy with a shudder.

"Think of that fly as our new best friend!" Andrew said. "Quick, get behind me and hang on! We're taking off!"

"That's a *disgusting* idea!" Judy groaned.

"It's less disgusting than taking a tour of Mrs. Scuttle's insides," said Andrew.

Judy got behind Andrew and wrapped her arms around his chest. Andrew tied one end of the Drastic Elastic around himself and Judy. He twirled the other end of the Drastic Elastic like a lasso and swung it toward the head of the fly. It wrapped around behind the fly's gigantic eyes!

Andrew tugged sharply on the Drastic Elastic. The next instant, Andrew, Thudd, and Judy snapped to a hairy patch behind the fly's head!

"A fly *again!*" bellowed Mrs. Scuttle.

She dropped the toast, and the fly zoomed off. Andrew felt like a jet pilot! The wind pushed them into the hairs behind the fly's head. The kitchen was a dizzy blur of colors and shapes.

Bzzzzz . . .

The fly's wings were buzzing right behind them!

Mrs. Scuttle's angry voice boomed below. "Wait till I get my fly swatter!" she said.

The fly zigged and zagged and roller-coastered around the room.

I was getting hungry, thought Andrew, *but I'm sure glad I haven't eaten anything.*

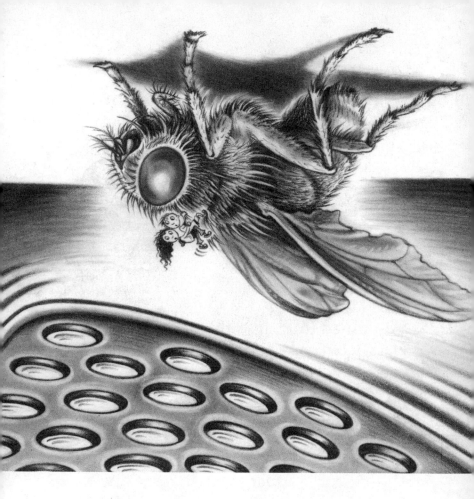

Then the fly came to a jolting stop!
Andrew and Judy would have flown off the
fly's back if they hadn't been held on by the
Drastic Elastic. The fly was upside down!

"Andrew!" said Judy. "We're on the ceiling!"

"Wowzers!" said Andrew. "I always wondered how flies landed upside down!"

meep . . . "Flying fly put up front legs," said Thudd. "Front legs stick to ceiling. Then rest of fly stick to ceiling! What happen to duck that fly upside down? Quack up! Hee hee!"

Andrew sighed. "I guess you're not totally cured yet."

"*Eeeyaaah!*" screamed Mrs. Scuttle.

They looked down. Mrs. Scuttle was coming after them, waving her yellow fly swatter! "I'll get rid of these filthy beasts if it's the last thing I do!"

The fly zinged off the ceiling like an arrow from a bow. A second later, they slammed to a stop. When Andrew's head stopped spinning, he saw green leaves. He was looking into Mrs. Scuttle's yard! The fly had landed on Mrs. Scuttle's screen door.

Behind them, Mrs. Scuttle was swishing the fly swatter.

"Gotcha now!" yelled Mrs. Scuttle.

The yellow blur of the fly swatter was coming straight at them!

We didn't drown in Mrs. Scuttle's bathtub, thought Andrew, *but now we could drown in squished-up fly juice!*

The fly zig-zagged across the screen door. It was heading for a hole in the screen! The fly folded its wings and squeezed through the hole!

The next second, they were flying at top speed through Mrs. Scuttle's garden!

I wonder if I have any Bug-Goo with me, thought Andrew. *If I do, I sure hope it's not leaking. . . .*

TO BE CONTINUED IN ANDREW, JUDY, AND THUDD'S
NEXT EXCITING ADVENTURE:

ANDREW LOST
IN THE GARDEN!

In stores April 22, 2003

TRUE STUFF

Thudd knows a lot, and what Thudd says is true! Thudd wanted to tell everything he knows about toilets and water and insects and eggs. But Andrew and Judy were too busy saving themselves from cockroaches and cooking to listen. Here are a few of the things Thudd wanted to say:

• Some people think that toilets flush counterclockwise in the Northern Hemisphere and clockwise in the Southern Hemisphere. But that isn't true. The way water flushes from a toilet or swirls around a drain depends on the way the toilet or sink or tub is made. It may take a while to find a toilet that flushes clockwise, but keep looking! You'll find one.

• All the water on Earth came from outer space! Most of it came from the giant meteorites that smashed together to make the Earth. And some water probably came from icy comets that later crashed into the Earth.

• The same water has been on Earth for billions of years. It gets used over and over. You may be taking a bath in water that dinosaurs drank! You may be drinking water that a caveman took a bath in!

• You can drink caveman bathwater because bacteria have helped to clean it. When bacteria eat the bad stuff in water, they break it down into harmless stuff that plants and animals can use again.

• Many insects have huge eyes. But their eyes don't see things clearly. Most of them couldn't see the letters on this page or even a stop sign. What insect eyes do best is see things move.

To an insect, movement says, "Danger!" A moving thing could be a hungry bird or a flapping fly swatter! Insect eyes can spot movement much more quickly than ours can.

• Many insects have eyes that wrap around their heads. This lets them see movement in front and in back and on the sides.

• Insects' antennas *feel* things move. So does the hair on their bodies. Yours does, too. For example, your hair tells you when the wind moves!

• Heating food changes it. For example, a raw egg has clear gooey stuff around the yolk. The gooey stuff is made of protein molecules. Protein molecules are like tiny machines. They have moving parts and jobs to do. When you cook an egg, the gooey part gets white and solid. The heat has broken down the protein molecules. They stick together and can't do their jobs anymore.

• You're made up of lots of protein molecules.

These molecules do their jobs best at your normal body temperature, about 98.6 degrees Fahrenheit. That's why high fevers are dangerous. The heat can cook your molecules!

• Butter is made from the fat in milk. If you got your milk straight from a cow, the milk would separate into two layers. The creamy fat would float on the watery part of the milk. That's because fat is lighter than water. If you whipped the fatty part of milk, it would form solid chunks. Squashing the solid chunks together makes butter.

Find out more!
Visit www.AndrewLost.com.

WHERE TO FIND MORE TRUE STUFF

It's on your teeth! It's in your nose! It's all over your sandwich! It's the weird, wriggling, microscopic zoo. You can see it in these books:

• *MicroAliens: Dazzling Journeys with an Electron Microscope* by Howard Tomb and Dennis Kunkel (New York: Farrar, Straus and Giroux, 1993)

• *Hidden Worlds: Looking Through a Scientist's Microscope* by Stephen Kramer, with photographs by Dennis Kunkel (Boston: Houghton Mifflin, 2001)

• *Yuck! A Big Book of Little Horrors* by Robert Snedden and Steve Parker (New York: Simon and Schuster, 1996)

Do you wonder how toilets flush or microwaves cook? Find out how all kinds of things work in this funny book (the pictures are great, too):

• *The New Way Things Work* by David Macaulay and Neil Ardley (Boston: Houghton Mifflin, 1998)

If you want to learn about bugs and see them in 3-D, check out this big, fat book:

• *The Big Book of Bugs* edited by Matthew Robertson (New York: Welcome Enterprises, 1999)

Did you ever find a potato that looked like it had a face? Can you make a banana peel look like an octopus? Would you like to make a pear look like a bear? Then you might have fun with this book:

• *Play with Your Food* by Joost Elffers and Saxton Freymann (New York: Stewart, Tabori & Chang, 1997)

Turn the page
for a sneak peek at
Andrew, Judy, and Thudd's
next adventure—

ANDREW LOST
IN THE GARDEN!

Available April 22, 2003

# THE BIG BUZZ

I guess you should never count on a bug to solve your problems, thought Andrew Dubble as he flew above the garden on the back of a fly.

Bzzzzzzz . . .

The fly wings behind him buzzed like a noisy engine. The wind whooshed against his face.

Sitting next to Andrew was his thirteen-year-old cousin, Judy. She was clinging to a hair behind one of the fly's huge black eyes. Andrew's little silver robot, Thudd, was hanging tight to the edge of Andrew's shirt pocket.

A few minutes ago, they'd almost become part of an afternoon snack for Judy's neighbor Mrs. Scuttle. Now they were zooming above Mrs. Scuttle's garden.

Kraaaack!

Mrs. Scuttle's screen door slammed.

"Disgusting fly!" yelled Mrs. Scuttle. She ran after them waving a yellow fly swatter. "I'll get you!"

Below them, Andrew and Judy could see a brick path. It led from Mrs. Scuttle's kitchen door to a cement patio with a picnic table.

All around the path was Mrs. Scuttle's garden. Purple daisies and pink lilies waved in the breeze. Rosebushes grew next to a white fence that separated Mrs. Scuttle's yard from Judy's.

"Look!" said Judy, pointing to her yard. "I can see your stupid Atom Sucker!"

The Atom Sucker was Andrew's latest invention. It had shrunk them so small they could take a hike on the head of a pin!

Andrew and Judy felt a gust of wind as Mrs. Scuttle's fly swatter swished by them. The fly flew in dizzy circles to get away.

Floating through the air were things that looked like spiky Ping-Pong balls. Some of them got stuck in Judy's long, frizzy hair.

meep . . . "Pollen!" squeaked Thudd. "From flowers! Make baby plants!"

"Oh, *great!*" said Judy, trying to pull the sticky things out of her hair. "I'm allergic to pollen! Ah . . . ah . . . ahhhhh . . . *chooof!*"

The fly swatter was right above them when Mrs. Scuttle let out a scream.

"Harley, *noooo!*"

Harley was Mrs. Scuttle's basset hound. He was standing next to the white fence. He was raising his leg!

Suddenly Andrew felt his stomach fluttering up to his mouth. The fly was going into a dive! The wind rushed against his face so hard he could hardly keep his eyes open. The garden turned into a green blur.

Andrew and Judy almost flew off the fly as it landed in the dirt. Their noses filled with strange moldy smells. On one side of the fly was a huge leaf bristling with hairs. On the other side was the brick path.

The fly crept along the ground. It stopped in front of a pile of shiny black goo and unrolled a fat hose from below its eyes. It dipped the hose into the goo.

meep . . . "Fly eating!" said Thudd.

"What's it eating?" asked Judy.

meep . . . "Oody not want to know," said Thudd.

"Yes I *do*," said Judy.

meep . . . "Bug poop!" said Thudd.

"*Eeeeew!*" said Judy. "Let's ditch this yucky bug!"

She started unwrapping the stretchy strands of Drastic Elastic that they'd used to hold them on to the fly. The Drastic Elastic was another one of Andrew's inventions.

"Don't tangle the Drastic Elastic," said Andrew. "We might need it later."

Judy finished unwrapping herself and handed the long loops of Drastic Elastic to Andrew. He snapped it like a yo-yo. The Drastic Elastic shrunk drastically. It was only as long as one of Andrew's fingers!

Andrew tucked the Drastic Elastic into the secret pocket under his shirt collar. He zipped the pocket closed.

"I'm out of here!" said Judy, sliding down from behind the fly's eye. Andrew followed her. Since they were as light as dust, they floated gently down.

Suddenly a scream rattled Andrew's ears.

"Cheese Louise!" Judy hollered. "This is more disgusting than when we were flushed down the toilet!"

A STEPPING STONE BOOK™

Great stories by great authors . . .
for fantastic first reading experiences!

Grades 1–3

FICTION

Duz Shedd series
  by Marjorie Weinman Sharmat
Junie B. Jones series by Barbara Park
Magic Tree House® series
  by Mary Pope Osborne
Marvin Redpost series by Louis Sachar
Mole and Shrew books
  by Jackie French Koller
Tooter Tales books by Jerry Spinelli

The Chalk Box Kid
  by Clyde Robert Bulla
The Paint Brush Kid
  by Clyde Robert Bulla
White Bird by Clyde Robert Bulla

NONFICTION

Magic Tree House® Research Guid
  by Will Osborne and
  Mary Pope Osborne

Grades 2–4

A to Z Mysteries® series by Ron Roy
Aliens for . . . books
  by Stephanie Spinner & Jonathan Etra
Julian books by Ann Cameron
The Katie Lynn Cookie Company series
  by G. E. Stanley
The Case of the Elevator Duck
  by Polly Berrien Berends
Hannah by Gloria Whelan
Little Swan by Adèle Geras
The Minstrel in the Tower
  by Gloria Skurzynski

Next Spring an Oriole
  by Gloria Whelan
Night of the Full Moon
  by Gloria Whelan
Silver by Gloria Whelan
Smasher by Dick King-Smith

CLASSICS

Dr. Jekyll and Mr. Hyde
  retold by Stephanie Spinner
Dracula retold by Stephanie Spinner
Frankenstein retold by Larry Weinber

Grades 3–5

FICTION

The Magic Elements Quartet
  by Mallory Loehr
Spider Kane Mysteries
  by Mary Pope Osborne

NONFICTION

Balto and the Great Race
  by Elizabeth Cody Kimmel
The *Titanic* Sinks!
  by Thomas Conklin